SH'MYRA J

Beyond the Heartache

Navigating Life After Loss

Contents

I

Book One

"Beyond the Heartache" is a powerful tale of love, loss, and self-rediscovery. After a devastating relationship, she embarks on an emotional journey to rebuild her life. Through moments of deep heartache, she learns that healing is not a straight path, but a winding road filled with lessons, vulnerability, and growth. As she begins to embrace the unknown, she seeks hope beyond the pain, discovering that even in her darkest moments, she has the power to rise again. But can she survive?

1

When the World Stopped

Heartache leaves us shattered and struggling to find meaning. But beyond the pain, our journey lies with growth, healing, and rediscovery. We all make wrong turns in life, similar to missing a turn while driving. None of us are given GPS directions in life to be able to live a perfect life because there's no such thing. The good thing is that even in life you can still make a U-turn and get back on track. The key is to recognize you've made a wrong turn and understand that you can change your course again. Just understand that you can have a positive outcome in your life if you understand the lesson and turn back around.

You've been thugging it out every day, but deep down it still hurts. Are you tired? Of Feeling alone? And also not being there for yourself? that's loneliness when you don't even have yourself. Life requires us to experience emotions and confront challenges that make us wonder if it's all worthwhile. Even as we overcome trials and tribulations, we must be prepared for the next challenge, as life is full of twists and turns. I wish I could say that once you get through the storm, there won't be another one, but that would be false hope. Unfortunately, the next challenge will come, and we need to find the strength within us to face it and say, "Okay, that's not so bad." We need to find a balance between happiness and chaos and still genuinely smile through the pain. Life, can be heavy, and we may constantly feel tired, but it's possible to change our perspective and lighten our load to enjoy these moments.

You feel as though you don't need anybody else when you have a pure heart and show love selectively, but the people you choose do not return the same type of love, you can feel heartless. It's hard to keep putting your heart out there and not receive the same effort on the other end. Heartbreak can turn a good heart into a heartless one. It can take a long time to come back from it too. But that's life. If it is easy to choose the right person or friends without knowing the other person's intentions you can easily fall into giving more than they deserve. You have to love yourself first, not your family, men, or a woman, you should love who you are and who you are becoming and then it will be easier for others to love you back. I know it's hard to do and easier to just pretend like it's there, but most of us give love and neglect to circle back, mainly because we never received it. We are accustomed to receiving love to sell. To fully be you, you have to love yourself. The good and the bad. The great thing about self-love is that it doesn't matter when you begin the process; you can always establish this as your foundation once you start loving yourself. And once your foundation is solid, nothing can shake you.

You question yourself why you are here. Why do I have to go through this pain? why it can't be peaceful all the time? It wouldn't be life, life is beautiful but you have to accept the good and the bad of being beautiful. Sometimes in life, we need to find joy in life's terms. That's all about perspective. Often, we feel down and discouraged because things don't seem to go our way. But that's just how life works. Anything can happen at any moment-whether it's a great blessing or a major setback. We need to stop trying to control everything and focus on what we can control in the present moment. A big part of that is how we choose to look at the situation. Life has its ups and downs, but if we have the right perspective and live in the moment rather than trying to control everything, things will work out in our favor. Don't let life bring you down when you've been given the gift of living your life. You might not think you're good enough for life or yourself but to tell you from experience, there are times that you're doing your best in life to satisfy you and others but they seem to not think it's enough for them, don't stop. Don't stop trying because it doesn't matter that they don't see you trying it would only be bad if you stop trying and you prove their point. Not giving up is the best thing you can do in your life to see results that you couldn't see before. You are enough especially for your future.

Do you keep getting used by people? always feel taken for granted? hurt by people? using your heart to take you for granted? you have a good soul. you care about people, especially if they are struggling in front of you. You are willing to lend a hand and provide the hope and love they yearn for in that moment, but you never expect anything from them in return. Many times, we do things for people without really knowing them. It's okay to be a kind person, but it's important to be mindful of the relationships you build, because what starts as a kind gesture can become more because of the effort put in afterward. Just be yourself and understand that not everybody is supposed to accompany you into the next chapter of your life. Some people shouldn't even make it to the next chapter. If something makes you sad when it ends, it must've been pretty wonderful when it was happening. But truth be told, the world is so sad, everything ends, everything dies, but if you step back and look at the whole picture, if you're brave enough to allow yourself the gift of a really wide perspective, if you do that, you'll see that the end is not sad it's just the start of the next incredibly beautiful thing.

Overthinking, not because I want to be sad..I just feel too much, I value people, emotions, people and promises. It sucks because I didn't have anyone that understands me growing up, so whenever someone shows me the little bit of attention, I get attached and always end up getting hurt in the end. You can always tell when a good woman has been hurt too many times in a relationship, she'll go from communicating with you and talking to you everyday, to expressing herself and nagging you trying to get you to change certain things to going completely silent. And that's when you're losing her, she's slowly but surely detaching herself from you. Because anytime a problem would occur, she'd say something to you and nothing would happen, so she's done talking. It'd be a lot of work to break that silence, a lot of work that I don't think that other person would be up for. But if you loved her, that work would be easy, Don't be an idiot.

The one thing that had hurt the most…

Watching you give up
  Watched you gave up on those dry replies.
  Watched you slowly talk less everyday.
  Watched you slowly lose interest in me.
  Watched you slowly walk out of my life.

Sometimes the things you love don't always love you back, and you can give, and you can give, and you can give, and you can give, and you can give, and sometimes you get nothing in return, you get NOTHING. You came to realize you had to stop trying to explain yourself when you realized you was begging for an understanding that never came. So you tend to don't talk about what you're trying to heal from. I think the saddest people always try their hardest to make people feel good happy because they know what it's like to feel absolutely worthless. If you can learn to find the light in whatever dark situation you're going through and you can learn to laugh at the things that should make you miserable including yourself sometimes, that's how you win life. You are not grown until you know how to communicate, apologize, and accept accountability without blaming someone else. Maturity is being accountable and willing to learn. Who's the person that you care about the most in this world? so if someone came and took that person and put her in a cloud in the sky, and the only way that you could see that person again is if you build a tower high enough to be able to bring her back down or to be with her again, would you wake up tomorrow and wonder why you? or would you get to building ?.

She's not mad you weren't ready she's mad because she could've saved her heart from a pointless heartbreak. She's mad because she didn't deserve going back down a path she healed from. She's mad because you could've left her alone, she's mad because you tricked her into believing you wanted to be something with her, she's mad because she didn't deserve that again and you knew that, she's mad because she trusted you, she's mad because you knew that she was on her last straw and you still did that to her, she's mad because she wanted you to be different so badly. Sometimes we meet people to show them what true unconditional love is, and sometimes those people meet us to show us not to be so naive with that true unconditional love. And there's a lesson in that, hopefully that person goes on and treats somebody the way you treated them and hopefully you go on understanding that not everybody deserves the kind of love that you have. It's a lesson that where both people benefit but in the moment it feels like somebody used you, it's just life, sometimes we feel as though we lose but in the end we truly win because we helped another person see the light and they had to show us the dark.

2

Shattered Dreams

The dreams she once had slightly crumbled in her hands. slipping away through her fingers like sand. It wasn't just one single event, but the slow, relentless unraveling of it all she thought she could count on. The life she had imagined, the love she always believed in, the future she had planned—it was gone in a light, shattered like shreds of paper wanting to get rid of something hard to put back together. Wondering how it came to this, how the promises that were filled up in her mind with hope now felt like it was haunting echoes of a future that would never be.

It was as if a part of her died, but the world and the ones around her expected her to keep moving forward, to keep smiling. Yet behind the laughs, her spirit felt bruised, aching for something—anything to make the shreds whole again. But deep down, she knew that nothing could ever bring back what was lost. When people know they did you wrong, they avoid you and then we think their absence is because we've done something wrong to them but a lot of the time that's not the case, it's just they don't have the guts to communicate or apologies so it's much easier just to let it go.

dear heart, sorry for all the pain

"her loss" but I'm the only one suffering
  "her loss" but I'm the one that got ruined
  "her loss" but I get panic attacks every single time and I still
cannot hate him
  "her loss" but I couldn't sleep for days
  "her loss" but I'm crying every night
  "her loss" but I couldn't eat for days
  "her loss" but I became quiet and insecure
  "her loss" but I lost interest in everything
  "her loss" but I'm the one still praying for his happiness".

Every day I show the world a happy version of myself, deep down I'm broken, words can't explain this pain inside of me. I choose to stay silent so I don't disturb anyone's peace while trying to find mine. When you realize you have never been put first in your entire life but instead you are just that person that fills a void in other people lives until they don't need you anymore. It almost feel unimportant because everyone in my life can go days without talking to me or seeing me and that's how it has always been. Knowing that I couldn't do anything but try my best through it all, looking back as if I fell in love, I fell in love with him, no one else, just him, he gave me butterflies when I received a message from him, I smile secretly when I heard his name because I felt so lucky to have called him mine. Our journey wasn't perfect but it was ours, and I would've stuck with him until the end. I didn't care how complicated it got, I still wanted him, he were my person, he was the one. All I have seen was him, he completed a part of me, I loved him and always will. I hate this situation because I've been here before, and I promised myself that I would never put myself in this kind of situation again because it's torture, and yet I'm here again in the same situation, wiping my own tears. Women will put aside their happiness for their man, but a man will put aside his women for his own happiness.

You try so hard to distract yourself but you still have this void in your heart, just want to know if that person ever regrets treating you the way they did. My absence never bothered you while yours destroyed mine, that was the difference between us two. It feels like my heart is frozen knowing I'll always be the girl people use and pretend to love until their happy and find someone better to replace me with. Acting like I don't care and like I'm cold, knowing I'm the most loving person with the purest love but this generation forces me to hide that part of me. Asking myself, "Is it worth telling someone else what you're going through" because all they would say is "You're strong and it's going to be okay" when you know it's not. The biggest and hardest thing I had to accept was that no one was scared of losing me.

I thought it was us against the world, but somewhere along the way, it became him against me. The same person who told me we were going to have kids together, that's the same person who told me he'd find a way to convince my dad, the same person who held me in his arms, the same person who couldn't go to sleep unless I was on call, the same person who promised forever, the same person who I would have given up the whole world for..now all of a sudden I wasn't enough. If I held on to him, it hurts, but if I let go, it hurts even more. It leaves me with the question, "Do I miss that person?" yes, actually I do.

I miss the person I fell so deeply in love with, but it's hard to not miss that person. The person I knew before is a person I could never live without. He's an entirely different person now, I don't know what made him change, I held on for months, hoping that they would still be here. But there's only so much a person can hold onto before giving up, and I'm quite sure he isn't going to come back anyway. I tried giving him my best and it wasn't enough and that's fine. I will forever be in love with the person he was and confused about how someone can change from the sweetest person to someone you can't even look at sometimes.

I didn't know what we were anymore, I didn't understand it, sometimes we're good, sometimes we're on bad terms, and sometimes we're just strangers. One minute you talk as if I was something special to you, and one minute you talk to me as If I completely meant nothing to you... don't play with my feelings. When he failed to understand the reason for my silence, I wasn't moody or full of attitude, i was deeply hurt. The twisted thing is that person might have hurt me more than anyone ever has, but that person loved me better than anyone ever did, too. Homesick for arms that don't want to hold me anymore. When I made a mistake, It was always bashed and spoken upon wanting to torture my feelings so I would never forget, but when you made a mistake, I forgave you, and still loved you even when it's something I would have never done to you... can you see the difference now? I trusted you, told my mother about you: prayed for you, waited for my birthday wish from you, told you about my feelings and problems, showed you my scars, sent you voice messages, called you nicknames, and texted you day and night, cried for you, missed you every day, defended you when people talked about you and wrote you paragraphs which you loved in the beginning and promised you'll never leave my side to you leaving my side and air communications.

Even after breaking my heart I still believed you made me happy. No contact but I still wake up looking for your message on my phone. Swollen eyes. waking up, if you were lucky enough to sleep, wondering if it was just a dream. Realizing that it wasn't, the pain in my heart reappeared. No "good morning" text, no, "I'm sorry I messed up" voicemail. Nothing. That was the new reality, a cold bed, an empty stomach and an ache in my chest that I fear will never go away. In a world that will forget you, tomorrow, never lose your mind and core values; hold on to the perspectives that keep your mind at ease and never try to please another human being. Never settle for less and try to be average. Push yourself to do your very best, not because we need any titles or rewards but because you and yours deserve the very best. Unfortunately, it's a proven fact if you don't push yourself you'll never be prepared for a world that could care less and not think for a second about putting you out on the street, it's a cold world.

You cannot stay in environments where people do not know your true values, if you stay in environments where people don't recognize your value, you will shrink your gift to the size of what they can stand, and that's what causes anxiety, depression, and stress. Because you had to shrink into a form where people can tolerate you, you have to refuse to be small because they think small. If you are in a situation where you find yourself not being able to express yourself, be yourself and relax your thoughts, dismiss yourself for the better. I have finally accepted that we will be strangers, and maybe one day we won't, but for now, I'm letting you go, I wish you the best and until we meet again, be safe, have fun, and dream big. But that doesn't mean my dreams weren't shattered in the process. There were times I wanted to say something that bothered me but I knew that it would have started an argument so I let it eat me up inside.

3

The Weight of Silence

The silence was deafening, It wasn't just the absence of sound, but the absence of everything she once knew—the laughter that used to fill every room, the comforting of every conversation, the warmth of connections. Now, it was as if the world had forgotten her, and in return, she was slowly beginning to forget herself in the process. Every spot they visited held a memory she wasn't ready to face. So she didn't. Instead, she let the stillness swallow her up whole, unsure that she would ever find her way out.

She hadn't realized how much the quiet could hurt until it became her constant companion. The silence wasn't just around her—it was inside her, filling the spaces where her voice used to be, where her hope used to live. She wondered if she could bear the weight of it for much longer, or if she would crumble under its pressure. She hadn't left the house in weeks. The idea of facing the world outside, of pretending everything was fine, felt impossible. It was eating her up inside, going outside to check the mailbox, and seeing the friendly faces of her neighbors, all seemed to belong to a world she no longer understood. Inside, the walls of her home felt like a sanctuary and a prison all together. She spent hours staring out the window, watching life go on without her, wondering if she would ever feel a part of it again. In another lifetime she thought.

She avoided phone calls, and the texts from concerned friends, unanswered. She couldn't explain the emptiness that sat in her chest, the exhaustion that clung to her like a second skin. How could they understand, when she barely understood herself? At first, she thought the numbness was a sign of relief. It dulled the sharp edge of the pain and made it easier to survive each day. But now, she wasn't so sure. The emptiness had become so familiar to her that it scared her as if it had taken a toll on her life that couldn't be paid for in full. She wondered if this was what her life would be now—a hollow existence where joy was a distant memory and grief was her only companion. The worst part was that she didn't even know what to feel anymore. Anger? Sadness? Regret? They all combined, but none of them took shape long enough for her to grasp. It was like trying to hold onto smoke.

She remembered how, not so long ago, the silence had been something she cherished. It was a break from the chaos of life—a moment to breathe, to think. Something unbearable. The silence broke me. It silenced me for a time. I cannot make you understand. I cannot make anyone understand what is happening inside me. I don't think anyone understands how tiring it is to act okay and always be the "strong" one when in reality you're close to the edge. When the feeling of depression kills me inside, and having to act like I don't care. Hurting, shutting down, turning into a total bitch I shut off my emotions, I act differently, towards everything and everyone and I hate it.

But that's the silence in me that overtook my happiness. The immediate urge to go silent when something upsets or hurts me, but the world and my thoughts already made me silent. Instead of expressing my anger or frustration, I simply withdraw and try to process my emotions in private. I accepted it already but it still makes me sad. Whatever happens, happens. I don't have much to say about anything anymore, it is what it is and life goes on. It's a different type of pain when you're sitting in your room at night time and suddenly you get hit by a wave of sadness while all you can do is suffer in silence. Silence means pain and tiredness of everything. Pretending to be strong and always okay is a facade I put on every day.

My body felt heavy, weighed down by the silence. Even the simplest tasks she does every day, making her bed, breakfast, and coffee—seemed to take twice the effort. Walking around like a stiff zombie with no expressions on her face. While her mind drifted in and out of the fog. Her appetite had faded, replaced by a constant ache in her chest and limbs. Not being able to sleep at night, weird dreams, fitful bursts, leaving her more exhausted than before. And even when she tries, the silence follows her into her dreams, haunting her with memories she could no longer touch. The silence was like a mirror she couldn't escape. It reflected on the things she didn't want to see: the choices she had made, the mistakes that had led her here. In the quiet, there was no one else to blame, no distractions to hide behind. Just her, and the reality she had tried so hard to avoid. Catching a glimpse of her reflection in the darkened windows, a shadow of the person she used to be. Was this her life now? The thought sent a shiver down her spine. She wanted to look away, but the silence wouldn't let her. It forced her to sit with herself, to confront the truth she had buried deep inside.

The saddest thing is, that the people that are most broken and that are hurting, and are the saddest, would do almost anything for anyone else because they know the pain. They know what it feels like, and they don't want anyone else to have to go through that. But in doing so, they break even more because nobody ever does that for them. It's crazy what a person with a kind heart, a pure soul, would do something for anybody but all they want is the same thing in return, and they can't even receive it. The only thing received back was a broken heart, tears, and pain because I just wanted someone to treat me the same way. It was a disturbing feeling low and then looking around and there was no one to hold on to. Good people are tired, to the point they get punished every time.

The advantage someone took of you to just fill a hole in their heart and leave yours even bigger. The phone was untouched on the counter, messages still unopened. Knowing people were reaching out, but just couldn't bring herself to respond. How could she explain her emptiness to anyone else? It was as if the more she withdrew, the farther away everyone seemed. She was alone in a crowd, lost in a sea of noise she couldn't quite hear. I lost most of me, all the happiness, all the joy, all the good stuff, that made me feel like I was nothing. Emotionally, I couldn't do it anymore, morally I felt exhausted, spiritually I felt dead although I kept praying and still having faith. Physically, I'm smiling for the family but that's just on the surface. Sometimes I want to scream to tell people how I really felt. Slowly, running from the silence wasn't the answer. No amount of noise and distractions could fill the void. She had to face it, sit in it, and understand why it had taken hold of her completely. It wasn't just the absence of sound—it was the absence of everything she used to know. And that was what scared her the most.

Maybe, just maybe, facing it was the only way out of the silence. If she should sit with the silence, and listen to what it had to say to her, then maybe she could have found the strength to let go of the past and move on. It wasn't hope, not yet, just something—a spark of possibility in the darkness that consumed her. Realizing that the person didn't need her anymore, and probably never will. And the moment that person tries to reach back out, she won't be there because how they didn't listen when she was there. Didn't hear her or answer her when she was there. She's not perfect, but at least she knew she tried, so now she won't expect herself to try when the person is ready. She's paralyzed.

4

Echoes of the Past

The past had a way of creeping in when she least expected it. A song, a smell, even the way the sunlight filtered through the curtains on quiet mornings—it all brought her back to moments she thought she had buried. But no matter how deeply she tried to hide them, the memories always found a way out. They whispered to her in the quiet, subtle, and persistent, like ghosts, she couldn't shake off. There were days when she could almost ignore them, pretending that the echoes were nothing more than a fleeting thought. But today was not one of those days. The memories were everywhere, filling the empty spaces in her mind and dragging her back to a time before everything changed—back to when she believed in love, in promises that now felt like lies on top of lies.

Started with a photograph she stumbled across while cleaning out her old book bag full of items she hadn't opened up in months. Her fingers brushed over the picture slowly, remembering the time they once took the picture in the mall by someone who stopped them and gave them a free frame and all. It was a picture from better times—laughing faces, arms wrapped around one another, eyes filled with hope while walking with him on his break. She stared at it for a moment, feeling the weight of it settling in her chest. How could something so small hold so much of the past? before she knew it, more memories came rushing in. The sound of his voice on a lazy Saturday morning after they just got done doing grown activities, loving on each other. The way they used to share sad moments, quiet moments, happy moments, wrapped in the comfort of each other's presence. Each memory felt like a sharp tug, pulling further and further from the present, back to the time when the future seemed brighter and the hurt she now carries was unimaginable.

The memories didn't just bring back the good—they brought back the hurt in her too that was stored away. The fights, the broken promises, the quiet moments when she felt the distance growing between them, even when they sat by each other side. She remembered how she used to brush those feelings aside, convincing herself it was just a phase in life, and that things always get better. But now, looking back, she could see the cracks that had always been there, slowly widening over time. A wave of regret washed over her. Had she missed the signs? Could she have done something differently? The questions echoed in her head, relentless and unforgiving. But it was just too late for answers—the past was out of her reach, and all she was left with were the echoes.

She closed her eyes, and in an instant, she was back in that moment—the day everything happened that she couldn't seem to get over. They were sitting in the car after a disagreement with her brother, the person, and her. The words they both said were echoing in her mind, sharp and final: "This the last time you going to hear from me". She was stubborn, but she wasn't the only one in the wrong, although it took her time to cool down and take accountability for what she said. The person also was stubborn right along with her. At the time, she had felt her world crumble around her, the words like a knife cutting through everything they had built. She had pleaded, tried to understand, but the expression on the person's face was set, his eyes distant, in that moment, she knew the person she loved was already gone, and there was nothing she could do to bring them back together.

The past held her in its grip refusing to let go. Every time she thought she was so close to moving on, something pulled her back, reminding her of the life she used to have. She wondered if she would ever be free from it if the echoes would ever fade. Part of her didn't want them to. As painful as the memories were, they were all she had left of that time—of the love that once meant everything to her. Letting go felt like losing all over again, like giving up the only connection she had left of that person she used to be. But somewhere, deep down, she knew that the past wasn't where she belonged. As much as she clung to them memories, they were nothing more than shadows now, unable to offer her the warmth or comfort she longed for. She couldn't go back to them, no matter how much she wished it to.

Each memory felt heavier than the last, like stones she had been carrying for far too long. At first, they were a comfort— a way to stay connected to the life she used to have. To the person she used to be, but no, they weighed her down, keeping her stuck in a place she no longer needed to be in. The more she tried to hold onto them, the more they slipped through her small little fingers. Leaving her with nothing but an ache, she wondered how long could she carry the burden before it broke her completely.

And then, in the aftermath of the memories, something stirred inside her—a faint glimpse of light, barely noticeable but there all the same. The past didn't just live in her mind—it overwhelmed her senses. She could smell the faint scent of his cologne, lingering in the air like a ghost she couldn't take on. The fabric of her favorite sweater felt like his touch, a reminder of all the times they sat close to each other, hands brushed up against each other. Memories shooting across her mind, hearing his voice, seeing his actions and nice gestures they both used to have together. Every sensation was a reminder that the past was still very much alive in her body, refusing to fade quickly into the background.

Maybe the time had come for her to face the truth: the person she used to be was gone, just like the life she used to own. And as hard as it was for her to accept it, she knew that if she ever wanted to find herself again, she would have to let the echoes fade, one by one. She wasn't ready to let go—not yet. But maybe, for the first time, she was ready to start trying to let go. The echoes of her past would always be there, she knew that much. But she didn't have to let them control who she was as a person. Slowly, she opened her eyes, taking in the quiet stillness of the room around her. The past was behind her, and somewhere ahead, the future waited for her. She just had to be brave enough to reach for it. You have to build your self-esteem. You can't outsource it.

5

Cracks In the Armor

She always prided herself on her strength, on her ability to keep everything together no matter what life threw her way. The armor she wore wasn't visible, but it was there—a protective layer she built over the years to shield herself from the hurt that always seemed to find her. It kept her sane in the world at a safe of distractions, kept her emotions neatly contained behind a wall no one could even breach. She thought it made her invincible, untouchable. But now, the first time, she could feel the cracks forming, spreading through her armor like fine spiderwebs all around.

It started with a small moment she couldn't control—a tear she didn't see coming, a sharp breath that caught in her throat when she least expected it. The armor that had once felt secured now felt so fragile, like it was only a matter of time before it shattered completely. No matter how hard she tried to keep everything together, the cracks widened each passing day. The weight of it all, the pain she tried so hard to bury, was pressing against the walls she had put up, threatening to break free.

She hated the feeling of being exposed, of knowing that the

people around her could see the cracks in her armor carefully constructed facade. Vulnerability wasn't something she allowed herself to feel alone. But now, with every glance in the mirror, every conversation that had touched too closely to the truth, she felt the walls caving in. Her armor, once a source a strength, had become a cage, trapping her in a cycle of denial and avoidance. Now that it was a breaking point, she didn't know how to stop it—or if she even wanted to.

Part of her wanted to hold on, to see if she could patch up the cracks and keep pretending that everything was fine. She wasn't ready to face the mess that laid beneath the surface—the grief, the guilt, the overwhelming sense of loss that had been chewing at her for so long. But another part of her, quieter but persistent, wondered if it was time to just stop fighting. Maybe the armor she had wasn't meant to last forever. Maybe, just maybe, letting it break would be the only way to heal the wounds it was meant to protect.

And then, in a moment she couldn't have anticipated, the armor gave way. It wasn't dramatic—no shouting, no flood or tears. Just a quiet collapse. She stood there, staring at her reflection, and for the first time in a long time, she saw herself without the mask she's been wearing for so long. The exhaust on her face, the pain, the vulnerability—it was all there, plain as day. The cracks had done their job, and now, there was nothing left for her to hide behind. For the first time, she felt the weight of it all, and she didn't have the strength to hold it back anymore longer.

The relief that followed her was almost as overwhelming as the fear she's facing. Without the armor, she felt exposed, raw, like a wound left open for outside elements to come in. But at the same time, there was a strange sense of freedom in it.

She didn't have to pretend anymore, didn't have to carry the weight of faking she built around her. The cracks had torn her wide open, but maybe that was the only way she could start to rebuild—not with her armor up this time, but with something real, something that could bend and stretch without breaking easily.

As she stood there, the remnants of her old self scattered around her, she realized something she hadn't before—she didn't need the armor. It had served it's purpose, kept her safe when she most needed it, but now it was time to let it go. The cracks didn't make her any weaker. They made her human. And maybe, in time, she could learn to be okay with that. She wasn't sure what would come next, but for the first time in a while, she was ready to find out.

For the first time in what felt like forever, she allowed herself to feel everything—the pain, the sadness, even the fear. It was uncomfortable, unsettling in her heart, but it was also real. There was no more in hiding, no more pretending like she had it all put together. And in that raw, unguarded moment, she realized that maybe it's not all so bad being vulnerable. That it didn't make her weak, but it was the bravest thing she could have ever done. She wasn't sure what the path would had lead her to, but she knew one thing: the cracks in her armor was not her downfall—they were her beginning.

6

Beneath the Surface

To annoy looking from the outside, she seemed composed—calm,even. Her words were measured, her actions deliberate, and her face rarely betrayed what lay beneath. But beneath the surface, where no one could see, was a different story entirely. There was a weight she carried, unseen by others, pulling her down every moment of every day. It was as if she was treading water, keeping her head above it all, but just below, the waves were crashing, and she could feel herself sinking.

The tension was always there, just beneath the surface—a constant, quiet pressure that never lets her go. It crept into her thoughts, her movements, and her conversations, making everything feel heavier than it should. She knew she was holding on too tightly, but the thought of letting go, allowing her emotions to spill out where others could see them, terrified her. She had become so skilled at keeping everything so locked away that sometimes even she forgets how much was buried inside of her.

There were days, when she could almost ignore it—the fear, the grief, the gnawing guilt that twisted inside of her like knots she couldn't untangle. But those days were becoming fewer and farther between. More often now, those buried emotions clawed their way to the surface, demanding to be felt. She tried to push them back down, to smother them with distractions and denial, but they were always there, simmering just below the surface, waiting for a moment of weakness to rise up and overwhelm her.

The cost of keeping everything hidden was starting to show. The tightness in her chest that just wouldn't disappear, the restless nights where sleep was a distant dream, and the constant feeling that something was about to explode inside of her. She had spent long suppressing everything that now, her body was starting to rebel. Her hands shook when she was alone, her heart racing at the smallest hint of conflicts, and she found herself exhausted by the simplest tasks. It was as if her body knew what her mind refused to admit—she couldn't keep this up forever.

What scared her the most wasn't the emotions themselves, but the thought of someone else seeing them. The idea that someone might look closely, might notice the cracks in her carefully maintained exterior, filled her with dread. She spent so long building up walls, convincing herself that no one needed to know what was happening beneath the surface. Vulnerability felt like a trap, a way to invite judgment or worse, pity. And the thought of being seen as weak, as someone who couldn't hold it all together, was a fear she couldn't shake.

It wasn't a dramatic moment that broke her. It was quiet, subtle—barely noticeable to anyone else. But as she sat alone, staring at the rain tapping against the window, something inside her shifted. She felt the weight of it all pressing down on her, and for the first time, she didn't try to push it away. Instead, she let it come. The tears were slow at first, gentle, but once they started, they didn't stop. It was as if the floodgates had opened, and every suppressed emotion she had been holding back came rushing to the surface, surrounding her in waves.

Once the dam broke, there was no stopping it. The flood of emotions that poured out of her left her breathless, shaken. Grief, anger, fear—they all hit her at once, swirling together in a spiral of a storm that could no longer be contained. It was painful and raw, and yet, there was a strange relief in finally letting it out. For so long, she had carried those emotions alone, pretending they didn't exist, but now, there was no going back. The surface cracked open, and everything she buried away was pouring out, unstoppable and unrelenting.

When the storm finally passed, she felt hollow, drained, as if she had given everything she had just to make it through. But in the emptiness, there was a flicker of something new— something she haven't felt in a long time. It wasn't peace, not yet, but it was the beginning of it. She had always been afraid that letting go would destroy her, but now, as she sat in the quiet aftermath, she realized that maybe, just maybe, facing what was beneath the surface was the first step towards her healing.

7

The Unraveling

The unraveling of her relationship hadn't been sudden. It started as small, imperceptible shifts—conversations that felt forced, silences that lingered too long. At first, she told herself it was normal, just a phase, something they could work through, but over time, the space between them grew wider, the distance deeper, until she could no longer pretend everything was fine. What once felt like a partnership now felt like two people living parallel lives, slowly drifting apart.

Beneath the surface, there was so many things left unsaid. She could feel the weight of those unspoken words pressing on her, widening the gulf between them. She had learned to suppress her frustration, to keep her hurt buried, fearing that if she do let it out, everything would fall apart. But in doing so, she had created a chasm where intimacy used to be. Now, even when they were together, it felt like they were oceans apart, both too afraid to speak the truth of what was happening.

She had spent so much time trying to be the glue that held them together, but now, she felt like she was breaking under the weight of it. Every argument they tried to avoid, every issue they left unresolved, piled on top of her, until she could hardly catch air. It was as if she carrying the burden of the relationship on her own, while he remained distant, detached, unaware of the toll it was taking on her. She couldn't do it anymore—she was unraveling, and so was their connection.

The silence between them had become deafening. It wasn't the kind of silence that brought peace—it was the kind that suffocated underneath them both, pressing in on her like a weight she couldn't escape. They had stopped talking about anything real, avoiding the topics that mattered, pretending everything was as fine like wine when it clearly wasn't. The longer the silence stretched, the harder it became the close to gap. She wondered if there was anything left to say, or if the silence had already spoken for itself they were too afraid to face.

It happened in a single moment, as most unraveling do. A careless mark, an offhand comment that hit too close to home, and suddenly, everything she had been holding back spilled out. The words she had swallowed for so long tumbled off her tongue in a rush—her frustrations, her disappointments, her fear that they had been drifting apart for months. For a moment, he stared at her, as if he didn't recognize the person sitting across from him. And in that moment, she realized with painful clarity that maybe he didn't.

In the quiet that followed their argument, a cold, hard truth settled over her: their relationship wasn't what it used to be. The love they once shared had faded, replaced by routine, by distance, by the avoidance of what really mattered. She had been clinging to the idea of them for so long, trying to preserve what little connection they had left, but now it was clear—it was already slipping through her little long fingers. And the more she tried to hold on, the faster it seemed to fall apart.

As much as she wanted to walk away, to let the unraveling take its course, something inside of her held her back. It was the fear of losing what they had, even if what they had was already gone. The thought of letting go of the life they had built, the memories they shared, felt like giving up a part of herself. But deep down, she knew that holding on to something so broken was only hurting her more. Still, the fear of the unknown kept her rooted in place, unable to take the next step, even as everything around her fell apart.

As she sat in the wreckage of their latest argument, she felt something shift inside of her. It wasn't peace, not yet, but it was the beginning of something. For so long, she had been fighting the unraveling, trying to stitch their relationship back together, but now she realized that maybe this breakdown was inevitable. Maybe it was what they both needed—the truth to be laid bare, no more pretending, no more holding on to something that wasn't real. It was terrifying, but it was also freeing. She didn't know what would come next, but for the first time, she was ready to face it.

8

A Glimpse of Light

She hadn't expected to find hope, but there it was—a faint flow on the horizon, barely visible through the fog of her pain. It wasn't the blinding light of a miracle or an epiphany, but something quite, more subtle. It was in the small moments: a deep breath that didn't hurt as much as the one before, a smile that felt less forced, the quiet assurance that maybe, just maybe, she wasn't as lost as she had once believed. The weight wasn't gone, but it was lighter now, and for the first time, she felt like she could breathe all over again.

As she took a breath and stepped back from the wreckage of her relationship, she realized something she hadn't before: she was stronger than she thought. The past few months had tested her in ways she couldn't have imagined, pushing her to the brink of what she thought she could handle. And yet, here she was, still standing. It wasn't perfect, and the wounds were still fresh, but she was beginning to see that beneath the pain, there was strength she hadn't known existed. She had survived the unraveling, and now, she was starting to believe she could survive any and everything.

For so long, she had held on so tightly—trying to control every aspect of her relationship, of her life, out of fear that she didn't, it would all fall apart. But now, in terms in the aftermath of everything, she was beginning to see that maybe letting go was the only way forward. It wasn't easy, but as she released her grip, she felt a strange sense of relief. The weight she had been carrying, the pressure to fix everything, started to lift. In its place, there was something new—a quiet freedom she hadn't expected.

Love, she had always believed, was about giving—compromise, and sacrifice. But now, as she stood on the other side of a broken relationship, she was starting to see it differently. Love, real love, wasn't about losing yourself for someone else; it was about finding a balance, about giving and receiving in equal measure. It was about respect, trust, and being her true self. She understood that love wasn't suppose to hurt like this. The love she deserved was out there, waiting for her—she just had to be ready to embrace it.

Without the constant strain of her relationship weighing her down, she found herself with time—time to think, breath, and reconnect with who she really was. It's been long since she had thought about her own needs, her own dreams. Little by little, she began to remember the things she used to love—car rides to places she loved to visit, library's she loved to go to, parts of herself she had neglected for too long. She hadn't realized how much she had lost until now, as she started to reclaim the pieces of herself she had given up.

The future was still uncertain, she still love him with all her heart. She had spent so long trying to plan every detail, to control every outcome, but now, she was beginning to embrace the unknown. There was a strange beauty in it—the idea that anything could happen, that she was free to shape her own destiny without the constraints of her past holding her back. She didn't know where she was headed, but that was okay. Uncertainty felt less like a threat and more like a blank canvas, waiting for her to paint something new, even if it was with him.

There it was—a glimpse of light, real and undeniable. It wasn't overwhelming, but it was there in a small moment: the warmth of the sun on her face as she walked outside, the sound of laughter with him she hadn't spoken to in weeks, the feeling of peace that settled over her as she sat down in front of him at dinner. These moments, however fleeting, reminded her that there was still joy to be found, even in the midst of healing. The light might have been small, but it was growing, and she was ready to follow it.

As she stood at the edge of the unknown, she knew her journey was far from over. There would be hard days ahead, moments when the darkness might return, but now, she had something she hadn't before—a glimpse of light, a reminder that healing was possible. She wasn't walking this path blindly anymore. With each step she took, she moved closer to herself, to the person she was meant to be. She didn't know where this road would lead, but she knew she was ready to take the next step—and that was enough.

9

Shadows and Secrets

Secrets have a way of weighing you down, even when you've convinced yourself they're safely hidden. For her, the weight had always been there, lingering just below the surface, shaping the way she moved through the world. She wasn't sure when it started—whether the secrets were hers to begin with or if she had simply inherited them from the people around her. But over time, they had become an inseparable part of her existence, like shadows she couldn't escape. And as they grew heavier, she began to realize that it wasn't the secrets themselves that would destroy her—it was the silence that came with them.

On the surface, everything looked fine. She had perfected the art of pretending—smiling at the right moments, speaking with just enough enthusiasm to make it believable. But underneath it all, a storm was brewing, and no amount of pretending could hold it forever. She had learned to wear the mask so well that even she sometimes believed it. But lately, it had started to slip, cracks forming in the carefully illusion. She wasn't sure how much longer she could keep up with it, how much longer she could hide the truth from the world—and from herself.

There were things between them that were never spoken of—small secrets, half-truths, and moments of doubt that they both chose to ignore. At first, it seemed harmless, a necessary part of keeping the peace, but over time, the silence grew even louder. She could feel the weight of all the unspoken words pressing down on them, widening the gap between them. She wanted to ask, wanted to confront the things that lingered in the shadows of their relationship, but she was afraid of what she might find. And so, the secrets remained, festering in the dark, slowly, eroding the foundation they had built.

The thought of bringing those secrets into the light terrified her. What if they couldn't survive the truth? What if the fragile threads holding them together unraveled the moment everything was laid bare? She had spent long time avoiding the uncomfortable conversations, sidestepping of their relationship, that she wasn't sure she could handle the explosion. Yet, the longer she kept them hidden, the more toxic they became, poisoning everything from within. She knew they couldn't stay buried forever, but the fear of what would happen if she unearthed them was paralyzing.

It happened slowly, almost imperceptibly at first—a stray comment, a glance that lingered too long, a text message that wasn't meant for her. And then, like a dam breaking, the truth began to pour out. She had known, deep down, that something wasn't right, but she had buried that knowledge, too afraid to confront it. Now, as the secrets she had been avoiding finally came to light, there was no turning back. The shadows receded, and what was left was the harsh, undeniable truth—ugly, painful, and impossible to ignore.

With the truth laid bare, she could finally see the damage that had been done. Every secret, every lie, had chipped away at the foundation of their relationship, until there was nothing left but ruins. She had thought she was protecting herself, protecting them, by keeping these things hidden, but now she understood that the real damage had been done in silence. The secrets hadn't just hurt her—they had eroded everything they had built, leaving her standing in the wreckage, wondering how it had all come to this.

Forgiveness seemed impossible, and yet, she knew it was the only way forward. Whether it was forgiveness for herself, for the secrets she had kept, or for him, for the ones he had hidden, she wasn't sure. But she knew that holding onto the weight of it all would only continue to pull her under. Letting go of the anger, the hurt, the betrayal—it felt like an insurmountable task, but maybe, just maybe, it was the first step towards her healing process. Forgiveness didn't mean forgetting, but perhaps it meant freeing herself from the shadows she had lived in for too long.

The shadows still lingered, but now, she could see a way out. It wouldn't be easy—there were still wounds that needed to heal, conversations that needed to be had, and truths that would take time to process. But she was ready. Ready to step out of the darkness, ready to face whatever came next with her eyes wide open. The secrets had held her back for too long, but now, she determined to move forward, to find her way toward the light, even if the path was uncertain.

10

The Turning Tide

There was a moment, a breath of air that felt different from the ones before it. She couldn't pinpoint exactly when it happened, but something had changed. The current that had once pulled her under was losing its grip, and in its place, there was a new kind of energy—a quiet strength that began to rise within her. It wasn't dramatic, not a sudden wave of clarity or a revelation, but something subtler. The tide was turning, and though she didn't know where it would take her, she could feel the shift deep in her bones.

For so long, she had clung to the past—the what-ifs, the should-haves, and the weight of all the mistakes she thought she had made. But as the tide shifted, she felt herself slowly loosening her grip. The past no longer had the power to drown her. She was still scarred, still healing, but the pain didn't feel as sharp, the regrets not as heavy. She didn't need to hold onto them anymore. Letting go didn't mean forgetting; it meant making room for something new. And, she was ready to make that space.

Her voice had been quiet for so long, buried beneath the noise of everything she thought she had to be. But now, as the tide began to turn, she found it again. It started in small ways—a decision made with certainty, a conversation she didn't avoid, a boundary drawn with firm lines. Each time she spoke up, each time she chose herself, she felt stronger, more grounded. She had spent so much time shrinking herself to fit into the expectations of others, but now she was reclaiming her voice, and with it, her sense of power.

Change had always scared her, and even now, with the tide turning, that fear still lingered. The unknown was vast and daunting, a wide ocean she wasn't sure how to navigate. But there was something different this time. Instead of fighting the current, she let herself drift into it, trusting that whatever it led, it would be better than staying trapped in the past. The fear was still there, but it didn't control her anymore. Change wasn't something to hear—it was something to face, and she was finally ready to face it head-on.

It wasn't that she felt invincible—far from it. There were still moments of doubt, times when the weight of everything threatened to pull her back under. But now, she understood something she hadn't before: she didn't have to be invincible to be strong. Strength wasn't about never falling; it was about getting back up each time she did. And now, as she stood on the edge of this turning tide, she felt the strength growing inside of her, steady and unwavering. She could survive this—she could survive just about anything.

For the first time in a long time, she chose herself. It wasn't an easy choice, but it was a necessary one. She had spent too much time putting others' needs before her own, sacrificing her happiness to keep the peace. But now, as the tide shifted, she realized that she deserved more—more respect, more love, more from life. And if that meant walking away from what no longer served her, then so be it. Choosing herself wasn't selfish; it was survival. She was determined to survived this on her own terms.

The future stretched out before her, vast and unknown. There were no clear answers, no guarantees of what lay ahead, and for the first time, that didn't scare her. Instead, it filled her with a strange sense of excitement. The uncertainty didn't feel like a threat anymore—it felt like a promise. The tide was turning, and she was ready to follow it wherever it led. She didn't need to see the whole path ahead to know that she was moving in the right direction. All she had to do was trust the current, and trust the current, and trust herself.

As the tide carried her forward, she felt something she hadn't felt in a long time—hope. It wasn't blinding or all-consuming, but it was there, steady and sure, guiding her steps. The road ahead was still uncertain, and there would be challenges along the way, but now she faced them with a new sense of purpose. She had weathered the storm, survived the darkest nights, and now, with the tide turning in her favor, she was ready to embrace whatever came next. She wasn't the same person she had been, and for the first time, that felt like a good thing.

11

Steps Toward Healing

Healing could never began until she acknowledged the wound. For too long, she had buried it, pretending the pain wasn't as deep as it was, hoping that ignoring it would make it go away. But now, as she stood on the edge of the next chapter in her life, she realized she could no long hide from it. The wound was there, raw and unhealed, and it wasn't going to disappear just because she wished it away. If she was ever going to move forward, she had to face it head-on, even if it hurt. Only then could she begin to heal.

Blame had been her constant companion. She had blamed herself for staying too long, for ignoring the red flag, for not being stronger. When she stops and think about it, it's never the goodbyes that hurt, it's the flashbacks that follow. She had blamed him for the lies, the betrayal, the way he had slowly eroded her sense of self. But as she took her first steps toward healing, she realized that blame was a weight she could no longer carry. Knowing that everybody make mistakes, and holding onto that mistake did nothing but eat her up and made her look at him differently than who he was now. It kept her tied to the past, and she couldn't move forward while holding on to it. Letting go of blame didn't mean forgetting or absolving anyone of their responsibility—it meant freeing herself from the chains it had wrapped around her heart.

She had a thought, if someone that's in your life is treating you like one of many options, help them narrow down they choice, by removing you from the equation. Sometimes you have to try not to care so much even when you really do, because sometimes you can mean almost nothing to someone who mean so much to you. Its not pride, its self-respect, and trust you will not seek any positive changes in your life if you keep surrounding yourself with negative people, so stop giving part time people a full time position in your life. Know your value, know what you have to offer, and never settle for anything less but what you deserve. She had always been her own critic, quick to judge herself for every misstep, every moment of weakness. As if she begun the slow journey towards healing, she realized that she couldn't move forward if she kept punishing herself for the past. Healing required compassion, not just for others, but for herself. She had to learn to be gentle with her heart, to forgive herself for the things she couldn't change. Learned that she might not have to get to spend the rest of her life with him, but he got to spend the rest of his life with her.

Trust had been shattered, not just in him, but in herself. One of the hardest thing she had to do was grieve the lost of him who is still alive. She questioned her own judgment, her ability to see people clearly, to protect herself from pain. But as the days passed and she took her steps, she began to understand that trust didn't have to be an all-or-nothing proposition. She didn't have to trust fully right away, but she could start with herself—trusting her instincts, her resilience, and her capacity to heal. Little by little she rebuilt that trust within herself, she that, in time, she could learn to trust others again.

Truth is they won't even know she's hurt, because they never looked at her the way she looked at them, "Are you okay?" always the same question, "I'm fine" always the same lie. She ran from the pain that if she let herself feel it fully, it would consume her. But now, as she stood at the crossroads of healing, she knew that avoiding it had only kept her stuck. Life is going to get hard sometimes, but she have to get up and get her shit together. She either had to be a puddle or an ocean, people walk through puddles like it's nothing, oceans destroys cities. She didn't want to be a puddle. The pain was real, and it wasn't going to disappear just because she refused to look at it. So, she stopped running. She allowed herself to feel it—to cry, to grieve, to rage if that's what it took. And as she faced the pain, she realized that it wasn't as all-consuming as she had feared. The more she let herself feel it, the less power it had over her.

The truth is, putting up walls was the easy part, it's tearing them down that was far more difficult. She eventually went numb because you can't break a heart that's already been broken. She had lost herself somewhere along the way, caught up in the tides of a relationship that had slowly eroded her sense of identity. Anger is sadness that had nowhere to go for a long time. She found herself piecing together the fragments of who she used to be—before the pain, before the heartbreak. Her biggest toxic trait was she knew how to love, but she didn't know how to believe that she was loved. She wasn't the same person she had been, and that was okay. In fact, it was better. Healing wasn't about going back to who she was; it was about discovering who she was becoming. And she explored the things that made her feel alive again, she realized that this new version of herself was stronger, wiser, and more complete than she had ever imagined.

It confused her because she looked at life as, with the right music you either look at everything or you remember everything. Nobody said healing was going to be easy. Healing wasn't linear, and she knew there would still be days when the pain felt fresh, when the weight of it all threatened to pull her back under. Now, she saw those days as part of the process, not a setback, step by step. Each day, each breath, she had to reach—there would come a time in her life where she can finally get to walk away from the drama and from the people who created it. If you want to see what someone is afraid of losing, look at what they photographed. It hit her kind of hard knowing what she went through. But each day she felt something she didn't expect to feel time to time: peace. It wasn't perfect, but it was hers. And that was enough.

12

The Power of Surrender

She had been holding on for so long, clutching to the idea that if she just tried harder, if she just did more, she could have made everything right. But the tighter her grip, the more everything seemed to slip through her fingers. The harder she fought to control the outcome, the more chaotic it became. She used to think communication was the key, until she realized comprehension is, you can communicate with someone all you want but if they don't understand a thing you say, it's just silent chaos. She was exhausted—physically, emotionally, mentally. And as she stood, in the quiet aftermath of yet another struggle, she realized that all her efforts had brought her no closer to peace. Maybe it wasn't about fighting. Maybe it was time to let go.

The idea of letting go terrified her. It felt like giving up, like admitting defeat. Having anxiety and depression is like being scared and tired at the same time. The fear of failure, but having no urge to be productive. Wanting friends, but hate socializing, wanting to be alone but not lonely, caring about everything, but caring about nothing, feeling everything at once to feeling paralyzingly numb. Sometimes not socializing much is not called being anti-social, it's just not having the time for drama and fake people. She questioned herself what if she stopped trying to control everything? What if everything fell apart without her constant vigilance? But as the fear gnawed at her, there was another truth she couldn't ignore: holding on had already broken her. Her worst feeling wasn't being lonely but being forgotten by the person she would never forget. The need to control, to manage, to fix—it had consumed her, leaving her hollow and fragile. Maybe letting go wasn't about losing control; maybe it was about fixing freedom. Understanding this, the fear still held her back.

There came a moment when the weight of it all became too much on her to bear. She stood at the edge, looking out at the life she tried so hard to control, and in that moment, something inside her shifted. It wasn't a grand declaration or a dramatic act—it was quiet, simple. She let go. She released the need to control every detail, to manage every outcome. It wasn't that she stopped caring, but she stopped fighting. She surrendered to the uncertainty, to the unknown, trusting that whatever came next would come, whether she was ready for it or not. And in that surrender, she found a strange sense of peace.

Sometimes we might not want to heal, because pain is the only connection to what we had lost. She wasn't trying to figure everything out. She didn't have a plan, a solution, or even a clear direction. But there was calmness in the not knowing, a quiet relief in surrendering to the process. She realized that life had its own way of unfolding, regardless of her attempts to control it. And now, instead of fighting the current, she allowed herself to float with it. Trust didn't come easily to her, but in surrendering, she was learning that sometimes the most powerful thing she could do was to let go and trust that everything would be okay. It's okay to fight for someone who love you but its a waste of time to fight for someone to love you.

There was a freedom in letting go that she hadn't anticipated. The more she surrendered, the lighter she felt. The weight of control, of needing everything to be perfect, having to stop overthinking life like she has to have a answer to every situation and feeling. She figures it all out by messing up, making mistakes, by missing an opportunity, or by seeking advice and not taking it. Figuring out what's important in life and what isn't. Not knowing what to do sometimes, scary, but, its okay. Always trust your gut and know that everything will work out how its suppose to. Overthinking is just a painful reminder that sometimes she care too much. She's too caring to people who are careless when it comes to her. Paying attention to people who ignore her, making time for people who are too busy for her, attached to people who are on and off with her. She began to see that life didn't have to be controlled to be lived. There was beauty in the chaos, in the unpredictability of it all.

Surrender didn't mean that everything suddenly became easy. The hardest part about walking away from him, is the part where she realize no matter how slow, she goes he will never run after her. There were still setbacks, still moments, where the pain resurfaced or when things didn't go the way she had hoped. She has to relax, she can't control everything, have faith and hope things work out. Letting go a little and let life happen. Setbacks didn't mean she had to start all over again—they were just part of the journey. And with each one, she learned to bend rather than break, to flow with the challenges rather than fight against them. She didn't want love, she wanted to be loved.

Surrender had given her the strength to face the unknown, knowing she didn't have to have all the answers.

In the space that surrender created, she began to rediscover herself. For so long, she had been caught up in the roles she thought she had to play—partner, caretaker, fixer, protector. Without the need to control everything, she could see herself more clearly. Who was she, beyond the expectations of others? What did she want, separate from the roles she had been assigned? She go all in, keeps her word, give it her all, and go the extra mile while putting herself last for those she cares about. She rarely receives the same compassion, and effort in return and still continue to give freely.

Surrender had always seemed like weakness to her, a last for those who couldn't handle the fight. But now she understood that surrender was the greatest strength of all. It took courage to let go, to trust life even when it didn't make sense, to release the need for control and allow things to unfold as they would. Surrender wasn't about giving up; it was about giving herself the freedom to live without the constant burden of trying to make everything perfect. And in that freedom, she found a power she had never known before—the power of surrender.

13

Voices of Strength

For so long, she had quieted herself for the sake of the relationship. She had learned to suppress her opinions, to swallow her feelings, because keeping the peace had felt more important than speaking the truth. Now, something inside her was shifting. She was beginning to use her silence had come at a cost—her own sense of self. Her voice, once quiet and unsure, was growing stronger. She was starting to speak up, to express her needs, her desires, her boundaries. And with each word, she was reclaiming the power she had given away.

She hadn't noticed it first, but over time, the balance between them had shifted. He had taken up more space, while she had learned to shrink, to accommodate, to compromise—often at the expense of her own needs. It wasn't that he had asked her to, but somehow, she had fallen into the role of the one who always gave more. Now, she was starting to see the imbalance for what it was. A relationship couldn't thrive when one person held all the power. It required both of them to be strong, to stand as equals, and she was ready to step into that strength.

It wasn't easy for her to speak her truth. The words felt heavy in her throat, weighed down by months of silence. But she knew that if the relationship was going to survive, if she was going to survive with it, she had to be honest. She had to tell him what she had kept hidden for so long—how she felt, what she needed, what had been hurting her. As the words finally spilled out, there was a moment of fear, but also relief. She was no longer hiding behind the mask of what she thought he wanted her to be. She was being fully, unapologetic herself.

Her honesty wasn't met with instant understanding. There was resistance, a push back against the new dynamic she was trying to create. He wasn't used to this version of her—the one who spoke up, who didn't just go along with everything to keep the peace. The tension between them grew, but she didn't back down. For the first time, she wasn't willing to sacrifice her own needs just to maintain the status quo. She loved him, but she had learned to love herself too. And if that meant facing his discomfort or even the possibility of losing him, then so be it.

She had always thought strength meant hiding her vulnerability, pretending that nothing could touch her. Now, she understood that the greatest strength came from allowing herself to be seen, flaws and all. She told him about her tears— the fear of losing herself, the fear that they weren't as connected as they once were. It wasn't a weakness. It was an act of courage, a way of saying, "This is who I am. Can you meet me here?" And in that moment, she realized that true strength in a relationship came from being open, not closed off.

Setting boundaries had always felt foreign to her. She had believed that love meant giving everything, without limits. Now, she understood that boundaries weren't walls to keep him out—they were guides to protect her own heart. She began to draw lines where before there had been none, making it clear what she needed and what she could no longer tolerate. It wasn't about pushing him away; it was about protecting herself, about ensuring that their relationship was built on mutual respect. With every boundary she set, she felt her strength grow, and with it, a new kind of closeness between them.

As she stood firm in her newfound strength, she began to see a shift in him as well. He didn't understand her boundaries or her need to assert herself, but slowly, he began to respect it. At times. As much as it challenged him, it also deepened their connection. With each difficult conversation, each moment of tension, they were rebuilding their relationship on a foundation of mutual respect, one that allowed both of them to stand in their strength, side by side. But things always take a turn.

They were no longer two people playing their old roles—the giver and the taker, the quiet and the dominant one. They were something new now, as for now, something stronger. She had found her voice, her strength, and in doing so, she had made space for him to find his as well. Together, they were learning what it meant to truly love—not from a place of need on dependency, as she thought, but from a place of mutual respect and shared strength. It wasn't always easy, as she did know, but it was real, and it was worth fighting for, as she did try her hardest. Their relationship had become a partnership, where both voices mattered, and together, they were unstoppable. As she believed.

14

Embracing the Unknown

She had always been someone who thrived on certainty, who needed to know what lay ahead before taking the next step. But in this relationship, the future felt like a blank slate, full of possibilities but also full of unknowns. It scared her—the idea that she couldn't control or predict what would happen next. What if it didn't work out? What if the love they were building crumbled under the weight of their differences or unforeseen challenges? The fear of uncertainty, and she realized it wasn't just about the relationship. It was about her fear of letting go and trusting in something she couldn't see. Faith.

She had spent so much of her life trying to control the outcome of things, thinking that if she just planned well enough, if she could foresee every obstacle, she could avoid disappointment. But love wasn't something that could be controlled. It was unpredictable, messy, and full of twists and turns she could never have anticipated. She was learning that in her relationship, she had to let go of the need to know where it was going. She couldn't script their future. All she could do was show up fully in the present, trusting that whatever was meant to be would unfold in its own time.

As days passed, she found herself learning to trust the process. Not every day in the relationship was perfect, but that didn't mean it wasn't working. There were moments of doubt, of frustration, but there were also moments of joy and deep connection that reassured her they were on the right path. She realized that part of the beauty of love was in its unpredictability, in the way it unfolded gradually, revealing itself piece by piece. She didn't need to have a clear road map. What mattered was the trust they were building, the shared experiences that made each step forward feel more solid, even if the destination remained unknown.

Being vulnerable had never come easily to her. She had always kept a part of herself guarded, hidden away, because letting someone in completely meant giving them the power to hurt her. But as her relationship deepened, she realized that love couldn't exist without vulnerability. Embracing the unknown meant accepting that there were no guarantees—that she could give her heart fully and still risk losing it. But it also meant opening herself up to the possibility of something beautiful, something real. She chose to take that risk, to let down her walls, knowing that love required a willingness to embrace both the light and the shadows.

She wasn't the only one grappling with the uncertainty. He, too, had his own fears and doubts about the future. But instead of letting those fears pull them apart, they chose to face them together. They talked openly about what scared them—about the risks they were taking by giving so much of themselves to each other. It wasn't about having all the answers or making promises they couldn't keep. It was about choosing to trust each other, to believe that whatever came their way, they could handle it together. And in those conversations, she found a new kind of strength—the strength of two people walking into the unknown side by side. As they believed.

As she let go of the need to control every aspect of the relationship, she felt a weight lift her shoulders. There was freedom in allowing things to unfold as they were meant to. She didn't have to constantly worry about whether they were on the right path or if the relationship was moving fast enough. She realized that love wasn't about reaching some predetermined destination—it was about the journey they were on together, the moments they shared along the way. She was freeing herself from the pressure to make everything perfect, embracing the unknown. She was allowing the relationship to breath, to grow, to become whatever it was meant to be.

The more she leaned into the uncertainty, the more she realized that it wasn't something to fear—it was something to embrace. In the unknown, there was potential for growth, for discovery, for their love to evolve in ways she couldn't imagine. She didn't know what challenges they might face or how their relationship would change over time, but she knew that they were stronger for the journey they had already been on. The unknown wasn't a void to be filled with worry or doubt. It was a canvas, waiting to be painted with the colors of their shared experiences, their hopes, and their dreams.

In the end, it came down to a choice. She could spend her time worrying about the future, about the uncertainties, and what-ifs, or she could choose to love him in the here and now. She could choose to trust that the love they shared was strong enough to carry them through whatever the unknown held. It wasn't a blind leap—it was a conscious decision to let go of fear and embrace the possibility of something beautiful. The future would always be uncertain, but she knew that love wasn't about guarantees. It was about choosing to show up, day after day, and to trust that together, they could face whatever came their way. She was so sure of it.

15

Beyond the Heartache

The heartache was undeniable. It had carved its way through her life, leaving scars that she would carry forever. She could still remember the weight of it, the heaviness in her chest, the way it had consumed her, leaving her feeling like she was drowning in a sea of grief and loss. But as she stood here now, looking back on the journey she had been on, she realized that the pain, as unbearable as it had been, had also been her greatest teacher. It had broken her open, but in the breaking, it had also made room for something new—something stronger.

Healing wasn't a straight path. There were days when the pain still felt fresh, when the memories of what she had lost resurface, threatening to pull her back under. But healing, she had come to understand, wasn't about erasing the past or pretending the pain didn't exist. It was about learning how to carry it, how to move forward with it without letting it define her. Slowly, piece by piece, she had rebuilt herself. She had learned to live again, to find joy in the small moments, and to trust that she was capable of surviving, even after all she had been through.

What she once thought was her breaking point had become

the foundation for something new. Through the heartache, she had found a strength she never knew she had. There were moments when she had doubted herself, when she had wondered if she would ever feel whole again. But each time she fell, she got back up. And now, standing on the other side of the heartache, she could see that she was stronger than she had ever been. The pain hadn't destroyed her—it had forged her into someone resilient, someone capable of facing whatever life threw her way.

Beyond the heartache, there was life. She hadn't been able to see it before, when the pain was all-consuming. But as she looked ahead, she say that the heartache was just one chapter in her story. It had shaped her, yes, but it didn't define her. There was so much more waiting for her—a future of possibility, of hope, of new beginnings. The heartache had taught her that life was unpredictable, that nothing was guaranteed. But it had also shown her that she was capable of surviving, of thriving, even after the darkest moments.

Love had been something that she associated with pain, with sacrifice. But now, she understood that love wasn't just about the other person—it was about her, too. It was about loving herself enough to walk away when she needed to, about loving herself enough to heal, to grow, to become the person she was always meant to be. The relationship that had once defined her was no longer the center of her world. She found a deeper kind of love, one rooted in self-compassion, in forgiveness, in the belief that she deserved happiness, peace, and joy.

The person she was before the heartache no longer existed. She had been transformed by the pain, but in ways she hadn't expected. She was wiser now, more in tune with herself, more aware of her needs and desires. She had learned to embrace her flaws, to see her scars not as marks of failure but as symbols of survival. She was no longer the woman who had once been afraid of the unknown, of being alone, of facing her own darkness. She had walked through the fire and come out on the other side, not unscathed, but stronger, more whole, more at peace with herself.

Forgiveness had been one of the hardest lessons to learn. It wasn't about forgiving him for the things he had done, though that had its place, too. It was about forgiving herself—for the mistakes she had made, for the times she had stayed when she knew she should have left, for the ways she had hurt herself and him in the process. Letting go of the guilt, the regret, the what-ifs—it had taken time. But now, she was ready. She was ready to release the past, to let go of the weight she had been carrying for so long. Beyond the heartache, there was freedom, and she was finally ready to embrace it. She would never say she wished she never met him, nor will she ever regret him, because at a certain point in life, he was exactly what she needed, they grew together, even though they grew apart. So for that she say thank you. But has she really moved on from it as she say?

www.ingramcontent.com/pod-product-compliance
Lightning Source LLC
Chambersburg PA
CBHW040200160726
48006CB00014B/1836